THE
UGLY DUCKLING

by
Hans Christian Andersen

Illustrated by
Jennie Williams

Troll Associates

Troll Associates, Mahwah, N.J.

Library of Congress Catalog Card Number: 78-18059
ISBN 0-89375-128-6

1989
Campbell Soup
a.l

Among the reeds of a sunny little pond was a duck, sitting on a nest full of eggs. She had been there a long time. Now the eggs were beginning to hatch. One by one, the tiny ducklings climbed out and looked around.

"Oh dear," said the mother duck. "The biggest egg still hasn't cracked!" And she sat on the nest again.

Just then, an old duck waddled up and said, "It's probably a turkey's egg. Take my advice and leave it there."

But the mother duck decided to sit on the big egg a while longer. At last, it began to crack, and out tumbled the baby.

"How gray and ugly he is!" she thought. "Perhaps he *is* a turkey chick."

The next day, she took her new family down to the water. She waded in, and they all followed her—even the big ugly gray one. "He can't be a turkey," she said. "He swims too well."

Then she took the ducklings to the duckyard. She told them to be respectful, to quack properly, and to walk like well-brought-up ducklings. And they did just as they were told. But some of the ducks in the yard said, "What? More ducks? Aren't there enough of us already?

And look at that ugly duckling! He can't stay here!" One
duck flew at the big gray duckling and bit him!

Then the grandest duck in the yard came over and said, "My, those are handsome ducklings you have. All except the gray one—it's a pity he's so odd looking."

"He is not handsome," said the mother duck, "but he swims as well as the others. Anyway, looks are not that important!"

Soon the other ducklings felt right at home in the duckyard. But the ugly duckling was picked on and teased by everyone. And he felt miserable.

After that, things only got worse. Finally, the ugly duckling decided to run away. As he flew over the hedge, he startled some little birds, who flew off in all directions. "They flew away because I am so ugly," he thought.

That night, he stayed in a great marsh. And in the
morning, the wild ducks who lived in the marsh saw him.
"You certainly are ugly," they said. Then some wild

geese came. They were newly hatched, so they were not
yet handsome. "You are so ugly that we like you," they
said. "Why not join us and fly away from here?"

Just then, some hunters began shooting, and their
dogs splashed into the swamp. The ugly duckling was so
frightened that he hid his head under his wing. A huge
hunting dog came up, and showed his sharp teeth. But
then—splash!—he went on past. And the duckling sighed,
"I am so ugly that not even hunting dogs will bite me."

The duckling wandered along until he came to an old cabin. An old woman lived there with a hen and a cat. When they saw the duckling, the cat began to purr and the hen began to cluck. The old lady could not see very well, so she thought the duckling was a fat mother duck. "Perhaps we shall have duck's eggs!" she said. So the duckling stayed. But of course, there were no eggs.

The cat and the hen thought very highly of them-
selves. And if the duckling ever disagreed with them, the
hen would say, "Who are *you* to offer an opinion?" And
the cat would say, "Keep your silly ideas to yourself!"
But one day, the duckling felt like floating on the water,
so he told the hen about it.

"What!" scolded the hen. "You get these silly ideas because you have nothing to do! Start purring or lay some eggs, and you will get over it." But the duckling had made up his mind to go out into the world and float on some water. So he did. And all the animals who saw him made fun of him because he was so ugly.

When autumn came, it grew cold, and the duckling was even more miserable. Then one evening, he saw some beautiful white birds. They were swans, with gracefully curved necks. Suddenly, they gave a cry, and spreading their wings, they flew south to warmer lands.

As the duckling watched them soar into the sky, he felt very strange. He gave out such a loud, piercing shriek that he even frightened himself! "Who are those beautiful birds?" he wondered. "And why do I feel so strange when I look at them?"

Then winter came. The duckling swam all day to keep the water in the pond from freezing. But at night, the ice closed in, and at last he was frozen fast. A farmer saw him, and took pity. He broke the ice, and took the duckling home to his family. Of course, the children wanted to play, but this frightened the duckling. He flew

about and spilled the milk. He flew into the butter, then into the grain barrel. What a sight he was! The children laughed, the woman screamed, and everyone tried to catch him. But he flew out the door and hid in the bushes.

The rest of the winter brought even more hardship and misery.

When the warm spring sun finally began to shine, the duckling flapped his wings and rose high into the air. How strong he had grown! He flew and he flew until he came to a beautiful garden, where the smell of blossoms filled the air. The duckling saw three large white swans swimming in a quiet lake, and once again he felt very strange.

"I must go to them, even though they will say I am ugly," he thought. So he flew down to the water and swam toward the swans. Then, as he shyly bowed his head, he saw a reflection in the water. "Is that me?" he thought. He was not an ugly duckling any more. He was a beautiful white swan!

The other swans swam up to him and greeted him. Little children threw bread into the water and cried, "Look! A new swan has come! He is the handsomest one of all!"

He felt shy, so he hid his head under his wing. But he was happy, too! He remembered how he had been picked on before. Now he raised his head and rustled his feathers. And he said to himself, "I never dreamed of being so happy when I was the Ugly Duckling!"